A Museum Mix-Up!

"There they are!" a voice called out. "That's them right there!"

The entire class turned around, looking at the wing they'd come from. The security guard with the bright red hair ran toward them. Right behind her was an older man with wire glasses.

"I'm sorry. . . . Can I help you?" Miss Alcott asked. She stood up and put her hands on her hips.

"You certainly can," the man said. He adjusted his glasses on his nose. "I'm Mr. Whimbley, the curator at Simon Cross. I've been informed one of your students broke a priceless statue we had in our modern art wing."

The red haired woman stared down at Nancy and her friends.

"The River Heights students are to blame!"

Join the CLUE CREW
& solve these other cases!

NANCY DREW
AND THE CLUE CREW®
#39

Museum Mayhem

BY CAROLYN KEENE

ILLUSTRATED BY MACKY PAMINTUAN

Aladdin
New York London Toronto Sydney New Delhi

This book is a work of fiction. Any references to historical events, real people, or real places are used fictitiously. Other names, characters, places, and events are products of the author's imagination, and any resemblance to actual events or places or persons, living or dead, is entirely coincidental.

⑥❦ ALADDIN

An imprint of Simon & Schuster Children's Publishing Division
1230 Avenue of the Americas, New York, NY 10020
First Aladdin paperback edition November 2014
Text copyright © 2014 by Simon & Schuster, Inc.
Illustrations copyright © 2014 by Peter Francis
All rights reserved, including the right of reproduction in whole or in part in any form.
ALADDIN and related logo, NANCY DREW, and NANCY DREW AND THE CLUE CREW
are registered trademarks of Simon & Schuster, Inc.
For information about special discounts for bulk purchases, please contact
Simon & Schuster Special Sales at 1-866-506-1949 or business@simonandschuster.com.
The Simon & Schuster Speakers Bureau can bring authors to your live event.
For more information or to book an event contact the Simon & Schuster Speakers Bureau
at 1-866-248-3049 or visit our website at www.simonspeakers.com.
Designed by Karina Granda
The text of this book was set in ITC Stone Informal.
Manufactured in the United States of America 1014 OFF
10 9 8 7 6 5 4 3 2 1
Library of Congress Control Number 2013948655
ISBN 978-1-4424-9967-6
ISBN 978-1-4424-9968-3 (eBook)

CONTENTS

CONTENTS

ChaPTER ONE

A Work of Art

Eight-year-old Nancy Drew held the mirror in her hand, studying the shape of her right eye. She kept looking at her drawing, then back at her reflection. She wanted to get it just right. "I think my eyes look like bugs . . . ," Nancy said finally.

Her best friend George Fayne leaned over to see. Nancy had a point. Her hair looked the way it did in real life, but her eyes were big ovals with a line down the center. The lashes curled out on both sides, kind of like creepy bug legs.

"A little bit," George said. "The insides look weird. What do you call those things?"

"The pupils!" Miss Alcott said as she walked by. She was carrying a tray of art supplies. There were old coffee cans full of paintbrushes and rolled up tubes of paint. "You need to fill them out a bit, that's all. Good work, girls."

Nancy looked at her reflection again, then made the pupil a circle instead of a line. Miss Alcott had given her the perfect tip. The circle really did make her eyes look more real.

"Sometimes it seems like she knows everything," Nancy whispered to George.

Bess Marvin stood two easels over. She was hard at work on her self-portrait. Bess was Nancy's other best friend and George's cousin. She loved fashion and design. Whenever they were in art together, Bess was quiet. She would work the entire class and never look up from her drawing.

"My mom told me that Miss Alcott studied in Spain for two years before coming to River Heights Elementary," George said.

"No way," Nancy whispered. "I heard she plays the guitar too. Hannah thought she saw a poster for her band at the music club downtown."

The girls watched their teacher move around the classroom, weaving between easels. She dropped off a few pencils and erasers to different students. Miss Alcott was the coolest teacher to ever come to their school. She had a purple streak in her hair and wore peacock-feather earrings. She was always showing the class famous paintings or drawings. Once she even brought in a collage she had done of New York City—where she grew up. The buildings were made out of newspaper and scraps of glittery fabric, which made them sparkle. Nancy had never seen a piece of art like that before.

Sydney Decker, a student at the easel beside them, seemed to be listening to their conversation. Sydney was supersmart. She always got As on her science tests and math tests, even when everyone else failed. "I heard she traveled all around Peru," Sydney chimed in. "She told Jess Ramos that she got her bag in Lima."

"Lima?" George asked. "Like the bean?"

"No, silly," Sydney said. "Lima—the capital of Peru. You know, Machu Picchu?"

Nancy and George shared a look. They had heard of Peru before, but sometimes it felt like Sydney was speaking another language. Geography was one of her favorite subjects, so she always talked about different countries. Sometimes they would catch her looking at maps in computer class.

Robby Parsons looked up from his drawing. He wasn't very good at art, so his pictures always ended up a bit strange. His nose looked like a mushroom. His eyes were two different shapes and sizes. Miss Alcott liked to call his drawings "abstract."

"Do you know where she lives?" Robby asked. "It has to be somewhere cool."

"She lives downtown in one of those giant gray buildings," Nancy whispered.

"Yeah," George agreed. "We saw her when we were getting ice cream at the Scoop. She was going inside."

"Are you sure?" Robby asked.

Nancy almost laughed at the question. Of course she and George were sure. Together with Bess, they formed the Clue Crew. They were always searching for clues and were pretty good detectives. They helped solve mysteries around River Heights. Sometimes it was a stolen wallet or cell phone. Other times it was more serious. They'd once helped an old lady find a missing puppy.

"Definitely," Nancy answered Robby. "She was carrying two bags of groceries."

As Robby went back to his drawing, Miss Alcott set down the last of the art supplies on her desk. She glanced up at the clock. "We only have a few more minutes, so finish up your self-portraits," she said. "And I want to remind everyone about our field trip on Friday."

At the words "field trip," the entire class erupted in cheers. "Par-ty! Par-ty!" Robby chanted. His best friend, Kevin Lim, let out a few loud hoots.

"It's not a party. . . ." Miss Alcott laughed. "Though I promise we'll have a lot of fun. As all of you know, the Simon Cross Art Institute has agreed to let us tour and sleepover at the museum. We'll spend the night in their medieval armor wing."

"Do we have to bring tents?" Amelia Davis asked.

"Just your sleeping bag and pillow," Miss Alcott said. "And anything else you need to be comfortable."

"Like your teddy bear," Kevin laughed. Amelia shot him a dirty look.

"Those armor dudes are scary!" Robby yelled. "I went there a few years ago, and they all had these giant swords."

"What will we do there?" George asked.

"At the museum, we'll go on a tour and eat

at the restaurant. We'll draw and paint in the classrooms. There are so many incredible works of art there. I can't wait to show you the impressionist wing. They even have an early Monet." Miss Alcott looked so happy as she described it, even if the rest of the class wasn't sure exactly which artist she was talking about. They'd only had art class for a few weeks. It was hard to remember all the different names.

As the class ended, Miss Alcott went around the room again, collecting stray pencils and mirrors. "Make sure you get your permission slips to me by Thursday at the latest," she said. "You'll need them for the trip. Great job, Bess," she added as she passed Bess's drawing.

"You have to let us see," George said. She leaned over, trying to get a better look.

Bess pulled it away. "One minute. I have to fix my lips."

Nancy and George waited impatiently, ready to see the secret drawing Bess had been hiding from them the entire class.

"Come on Bess! We're dying to see it," Nancy cried.

Finally, Bess spun her sketch pad around, revealing the picture she'd been working on. The girl in the drawing had the same eyes as Bess. She had the same thick bangs and light shoulder length hair. She even had the same way of smiling that Bess did.

"That's amazing!" George said. "The drawing looks exactly like you."

Bess's cheeks turned pink. "Thanks. So . . . what did I miss?"

Nancy and George laughed. "Are you serious? You didn't hear anything Miss Alcott said?"

Bess shrugged. "I guess I was really concentrating. . . ."

"She reminded us about the field trip on Friday. Don't forget your permission slip," Nancy said. She grabbed her backpack and headed for the door with George. Bess tucked her sketch pad in her cubby, then followed behind them.

"How could I forget? I've been excited for the

last two weeks. Did you know that the Simon Cross Art Institute has a two-story mural in it? Or this room where you can throw paint on the walls?"

"That's crazy," Nancy said.

"It's a special exhibit!" Bess said.

"I've been saving my allowance," George said. "I want to get something cool from the gift shop."

The girls huddled together in the hallway. Nancy was smiling so much her face hurt. Field trips at River Heights were always so much fun, and now they were going to have one with their favorite teacher. "Dinner with Miss Alcott, a sleepover with all our friends . . . what could be better than this?"

George wrapped her arms around Bess and Nancy. "Nothing!" She yelled it so loud that half the hallway turned around.

Nancy laughed. Even if George could be a little silly, she knew her friend was right: Friday would be the best field trip yet.

ChaPTeR Two

Tour Trouble

That Friday, the girls and their class toured the halls of the Simon Cross Art Institute, following behind Miss Alcott. They had only been at the museum a few hours, but they'd already gone to the exhibit Bess had mentioned on Monday. It was a huge white room where anyone could draw and paint on the walls. They had stayed there for over an hour.

After that they'd walked through the sculpture hall and spent another hour doing ink drawings in the museum's classroom, a special area set aside for school visits. Now they were in a giant room with high ceilings.

"And this is the impressionist wing," Miss

Alcott said, pointing around. The light blue walls were covered with paintings and drawings of all different sizes.

"What does that mean again . . . 'impressionist'?" Bess asked.

Miss Alcott smiled. "I'm happy you asked. The impressionist artists were interested in light. They used small brush strokes that you could see if you looked real closely. They liked painting ordinary subjects like people or nature."

The class scattered around the great room. Some kids stood in front of a giant painting of a woman in a straw hat. Others looked at a wall of tiny paintings of boats. Bess, Nancy, and George looked at a picture of mountains and a sky. They could see each brush stroke, like Miss Alcott said.

After a few minutes, Miss Alcott waved the class over to a pencil drawing hanging at the far end of the room. "And this is what I really wanted you guys to see," she said. "When I was your age, I saw my first Monet painting at the Metropolitan Museum of Art in New York City. I remember how I felt. It was so huge and so beautiful. It changed my life. I know this isn't the same thing, but this is one of Monet's earliest drawings. Simon Cross is lucky enough to have it."

"The water lilies!" George called out. "I remember you showed us that painting."

"That's right." Miss Alcott said. "This is by the same artist. These are some trees he drew when he was starting out."

The class huddled around the small drawing, which was no bigger than a piece of paper. "This is so cool," Bess whispered to Nancy. "We have to see if we can get our parents to take us to New York City to see the bigger ones."

"Take another minute to look around," Miss Alcott added. "Then we'll go through the modern art wing to the museum's restaurant. Is everyone in the mood for grilled cheese sandwiches?"

The class jumped up and down and cheered.

Nancy was about to clap when a security guard
at the other end of the hall put his finger over
his lips. "SHHHHHHHH!" he said loudly.

Miss Alcott waved the kids out a side door,
then down a long hallway. "Whoops. We have

to remember to be quiet," she said. "It is a museum. . . ."

"I wonder what's in there," George asked, pointing to a door covered with a white sheet. A sign was taped to the front of it. UNDER CONSTRUCTION, it read.

"Look, almost this whole wing is closed!" Nancy added. The class walked past door after

door. Each one had the same sign on it.

They followed Miss Alcott out the other end of the hall, but not before stopping by a giant glass exhibit. A sign beside it said WILD.

"This is a new modern art piece," Miss Alcott said, pointing into the glass room. There was a black canvas on a wall and a few feathers on the floor.

"What is it?" Nancy asked.

"I'm not sure . . . ," Miss Alcott said. "Modern art can be a bit wacky sometimes." She waved to a security guard at the other end of the wing. The woman was playing a game on her cell phone. Miss Alcott had to clear her throat a few times before the woman looked up.

The security guard was short with bright red hair. She pointed inside. "It has a live ostrich as part of the exhibit. It's supposed to be about living creatures and art."

"I don't get it," Sydney said.

Miss Alcott shrugged, then pointed everyone through to the restaurant. It was almost six o'clock, and the dining room was filled with people. A few families finished their dinners. Another class was sitting at the far end of the room, talking with their teacher. The ceiling was covered with flowering plants.

There was a long table in the corner with nearly ten seats. A few feet beside it, a woman sat on a folding chair, playing a harp. The music filled the giant room. Waiters strode past with silver trays of food. Nancy couldn't believe they'd come to some place so nice—on a field trip.

"Everyone, have a seat," Miss Alcott said, pointing to the long table. Waiters came over, and one by one dropped plates of grilled cheese.

"This is incredible," Bess said. She looked down at the white tablecloth and napkins. Each kid had his or her own engraved fork and knife. There were vases in the center of each table with all different color roses. "How fancy!"

"Look at my dinner!" George added. She'd never seen grilled cheese like this. It was cut into tiny triangles. On the side of each dish was a glass cup filled with fresh fruit. There was a leaf of mint for decoration.

"I can't wait to see what the desserts are like," Nancy said. A waiter came around and poured glasses of lemonade or iced tea. Hannah, the Drew family housekeeper, usually didn't let Nancy have sugary drinks. As Nancy took her first sip, she felt like she was breaking a rule.

"I want a double-fudge sundae and sprinkles," Robby mumbled. He was already halfway done with his sandwich. His mouth was so full that they could barely understand what he'd said.

"Did everyone have fun this afternoon?" Miss Alcott asked. She sat down at the head of the table. Jenny Lynn was sick and two of the other kids from class had forgotten their permission slips, so there were only eight of them in all. Nancy liked how small the class felt this way, all sitting at one table. She had spent the whole time in the interactive exhibit talking to Beth Derth, a girl with two long blond braids. Beth's mom was the other adult supervising the trip. Because their last names were close in the alphabet, Beth and Nancy sat next to each other in a lot of classes before. But Nancy had never really gotten to know her.

"The best time," Beth said. "My favorite part was the ink drawings. I got half the bottle on my hands." She held up her fingers, which were spotted black.

"Me too!" George said. She held up her hands, and they looked the same. They'd used these funny fountain pens. Miss Alcott had put a bunch of objects in the center of the room for them to draw. She had called it a "still life." They all had drawn a picture of a bottle, a few feathers, and carved wooden box.

"And throwing the paint on the walls," Kevin said. "How is that not everyone's favorite part?"

Nancy laughed, knowing Kevin was right. At the interactive exhibit, the class got to put on white jumpsuits and splatter paint on the walls. By the end, the white walls were covered with neon yellow, green, and blue paints. They washed the paints off before the next class began their group masterpiece. Nancy still had some yellow paint in her hair.

"And the Monet drawing," Bess said. "I can't wait to see the armor, too."

"Yeah!" Robby yelled. "Swords and axes and stuff."

Miss Alcott smiled. "Yes, swords and axes. There's even a statue of a horse, complete with the armor it wore in battle."

Kevin high-fived Robby. "I can't believe that's where we'll be sleeping."

Miss Alcott pointed to a giant arched doorway off the restaurant. "After we're finished eating, we'll go look at the drawings in the—"

"There they are!" a voice called out. "That's them right there!"

The entire class turned around, looking at the wing they'd come from. The security guard with the bright red hair ran toward them. Right behind her was an older man with wire glasses.

"I'm sorry. . . . Can I help you?" Miss Alcott asked. She stood up and put her hands on her hips.

"You certainly can," the man said. He adjusted his glasses on his nose. "I'm Mr. Whimbley, the curator at Simon Cross. I've been informed one of your students broke a priceless statue we had in our modern art wing."

"I found it right after they walked through!" the guard yelled. "It couldn't have been anyone else."

"But we didn't do anything," Nancy called out. She couldn't just sit there and let them accuse her friends and Miss Alcott. She had watched the class the entire time they were walking through that wing. No one had left the group.

"Likely story," the guard said.

Miss Alcott's face turned red. Nancy had never seen her so upset. She looked like she might cry. "I promise you," she said. "We had nothing to do with that. I had the class together the entire time. They didn't leave my sight for even a minute!"

Mr. Whimbley crossed his arms over his chest. He looked around the rest of the restaurant, then back at the security guard at his side. "What do you think, Rita? Are you sure?"

The red-haired woman stared down at Nancy and her friends. "Sure as ever," she growled. "The River Heights students are to blame!"

CHAPTER THREE

Smashed to Bits

"I don't think you quite understand our problem," Mr. Whimbley said. He kept fiddling with his glasses as he spoke. "That sculpture was by a French artist."

Robby leaned over and whispered to Kevin. "Can't he make another one?"

Mr. Whimbley pointed a finger in Robby's face. "No, he cannot make another one. He cannot make another one because he's been dead for one hundred years!"

Miss Alcott's mouth dropped open. The entire restaurant turned to see what the yelling was about. A woman put her baby in her lap, covering the little girl's ears.

"I'm so sorry to hear that," Miss Alcott said, "But we really had nothing to do with this."

"Come with me!" Mr. Whimbley yelled over his shoulder. "All of you."

He strode out of the restaurant. The guard named Rita waved the children to follow behind in single file.

"He seems really angry," Nancy whispered to her friends.

"And Miss Alcott looks like she's going to cry," Bess added. "It's not fair."

Robby and Kevin were still laughing, even when they walked into the hallway. George nudged Robby hard in the ribs. "You're going to get us into even more trouble!" she said.

Mr. Whimbley walked four times as fast as everyone else, passing the closed galleries, the modern art exhibits, and a few sculptures covered in white cloth. The security guard walked in the back of the group, making sure all the children were there. When they finally reached the end of the hall, Mr. Whimbley pulled back a curtain, ushering them into a side room.

In the center of it was a tall marble podium. A huge clay sculpture sat on the ground beside it. It was of a woman's head, the nose and ears broken off. Nancy couldn't help but feel like it was staring at her.

"This is terrible," Miss Alcott said. She circled the statue on the ground, looking at the marble podium it used to be standing on. The sculpture was made out of shiny red clay. Red dust covered the white floor.

"Yes, it definitely is," Rita said. "There are more than five different pieces there! Smashed to bits!"

"It will cost at least four thousand dollars to repair this," Mr. Whimbley said. "And it will never be the same. Someone is responsible. The sculpture didn't just fall over by itself."

Nancy looked down at the statue. Bess and George stood close behind her. When the guard wasn't looking, she picked up one of the statue's broken ears. It felt heavy in her hand. Mr. Whimbley was right. It wouldn't have fallen off the podium. Someone must've knocked into it.

"So, tell us what happened, Rita," Mr. Whimbley said.

"I was in the hall outside, watching this group of kids pass through. Then I went into one of the side rooms because I thought I heard something. Within a minute . . . *BAM! CRASH!* I ran here, and this statute was on the ground. The curtain was moving. One of these kids must have run through here and left."

The entire class started talking. "How are you so sure it was us?" Kevin asked.

"None of us left the group—not even for a minute," Sydney added.

"Who else could it have been then? Your class was the only class in the entire hall. I'd been standing there for over an hour," Rita said. "I'm positive."

"It's a misunderstanding," Miss Alcott said. Nancy and Bess noticed her hands were shaking. They'd never seen her so nervous before. "Please, let's talk about this. I'm sure by the morning we'll have this all straightened out."

"There's no use in talking. We either need a time machine or four thousand dollars. Someone is going to have to pay for this. And if your students didn't do it, then who did?"

Miss Alcott opened her mouth to say something else, but Mr. Whimbley walked away. He slipped behind the curtain, turning once before going.

"Rita?" he said. "Will you bring the class back to the restaurant?"

The security guard nodded. Almost as soon as Mr. Whimbley walked away, Miss Alcott's eyes filled with tears. "I can't believe this is happening," she said sadly. "This is such a nightmare. What am I going to do?"

"I think we know how we can help," Nancy whispered to her friends. She scanned the room, looking for anything that seemed strange. "It's time for the Clue Crew to get to work!"

CHAPTER FOUR

A Puzzling Purse

"We can get to the bottom of this," Bess said, pulling Miss Alcott aside. "There has to be an explanation."

Miss Alcott covered her mouth with her hand. "I hope so. . . . But how? We don't have much time."

"Mr. Whimbley!" Nancy called. "Can we have one minute to talk with you?"

Mr. Whimbley brushed the bald spot on the back of his head as he walked. He didn't turn around.

"Please!" Miss Alcott said. She grabbed his arm.

"I don't know what to tell you," Mr. Whimbley said. He clapped his hands together as he spoke.

"The museum needs four thousand dollars to fix that statue. It'll have to come from the River Heights school district."

"You have to give us a chance," Miss Alcott said. "At least let us try to figure out what happened. I know my students didn't do this. It's a small class, and I was with them the whole time."

Mr. Whimbley watched as another group of students marched through the wing. They were walking single file, their hands on each other's shoulders. They barely looked at any of the closed exhibits. "Who else could it have been?" he repeated. "Dozens of classes come through here every day, but your class was the only class that came through right when the statue was broken."

"We're not sure who did this," Nancy said, "but that's what we want to find out."

Sydney stepped forward. "Nancy and her friends have solved every mystery in River Heights. When our principal's computer was stolen, they were the ones who found out who did it. They'll figure this out too. You'll get your money."

Mr. Whimbley looked at Nancy and her friends. "Aren't you a little young to be solving mysteries?" he asked.

"Trust us—they're good!" Robby yelled from the back of the group. "Nancy, George, and Bess can solve anything."

Miss Alcott clasped her hands together. "Please? Just one chance?" she asked.

Mr. Whimbley took a deep breath. "If you swear it wasn't you, I suppose I can give you until tomorrow morning. We'll meet at ten o'clock, before you leave. But no more. If you can't come up with some explanation for me, then River Heights Elementary will have to take responsibility. You were the last students seen in this wing. It's clear someone knocked the sculpture over."

"Thank you," Miss Alcott said. A few students were so relieved that they clapped.

Nancy knew they didn't have much time. "Can we go back to the room with the sculpture?" she asked. "We want to take a closer look at where it happened. That's the best place to start."

"I can bring the rest of the class back to the restaurant," Miss Alcott said.

Mr. Whimbley rubbed his forehead. "I guess," he said, striding down the hall. "Follow me."

While the class went to the restaurant, Nancy, Bess, and George returned to the room with the sculptures, and they went to work. They knew they could find out so much by searching the scene. Four other sculptures were in the room—one in each corner. The broken sculpture had been on a high podium in the center.

"Do you see that?" George asked. She pointed to the scaffolding covering one wall. A giant blue tarp hung over it. "I didn't notice it before."

"Someone could've been hiding in there," Nancy said. She jogged around the room. A man in a green jumpsuit swept the red stuff from the floor. Nancy knelt down to look. "It's dust from the sculpture. Like tiny bits of clay."

Just then Rita, the security guard, returned. "I thought I told you girls to get back to the restaurant!"

"Now, now, Rita," Mr. Whimbley said. "I'm allowing the girls to look around to see if they notice anything strange. Can you tell them again what happened?"

Bess stepped forward. She pulled a tiny sketch pad from her knapsack. "It would help us a lot," she said.

Rita didn't look pleased. Still, she cleared her throat and began. "I was standing near the sculpture, and I went into one of the closed galleries for a moment because I thought I heard a sound. There was nothing in the first gallery, then *CRASH!* When I got here, the sculpture was turned over. Smashed on the floor. Then I saw that curtain right there moving, like someone had just left." She pointed to the doorway beside the scaffolding.

Bess scribbled down notes in her sketch pad. "That's all helpful," she said.

Nancy took another walk around the room as the janitor swept up the last of the red dust. "The red dust was on this side of the podium, which meant the person hit the sculpture from this side." She pointed to the side closest to Rita.

"Wait! I found something!" Bess called from across the room. She held a purple coin purse in the air. "It was right beneath the tarp. Someone must've dropped it."

George and Nancy ran to her and studied the purse. There were tiny flowers on the front of it. It looked like it belonged to someone their age.

"Does it look familiar?" Mr. Whimbley asked. "Maybe it belongs to one of your classmates."

"Maybe, but I've never seen it before," Nancy said. She plucked it from Bess's hand and then turned it over. On the back was a sticker that said BENSONHURST ACADEMY. "This is a school two towns over. Are they visiting today?"

Mr. Whimbley adjusted his glasses, trying to read the fine print. "Yes, I think they are."

"But which student could it belong to?" George asked. "Is there anything inside?"

Nancy opened up the wallet. There were only a few coins. "Well, whoever dropped it will come back here looking for it. That's for sure."

"And even if they're not the person who broke the sculpture," George said. "They may have seen something."

"Are you thinking what I'm thinking?" Bess asked.

"What are you thinking?" Mr. Whimbley said, crossing his arms over his chest.

"We'll have to have a stake out," Nancy said.

The girls all split up, ignoring Rita and Mr. Whimbley. They had more important things to do. They had to find the perfect place to hide.

ChaPTER FiVE

Stake Out

"Ow," Bess moaned. She shook her foot several times. "My foot is asleep. I don't know how much longer I can stay here."

"Shh!" George whispered. "We're close. I can feel it."

The room was dark. The girls were all squished behind another statue, a weird blob that looked like an elephant. The woman's head from the broken statue still lay on the floor. In the dim light, the tarp looked like a giant ghost. "Whoever this belongs to will have to come back eventually, right?" Nancy asked.

She was starting to feel unsure. Mr. Whimbley

and Rita had agreed to let them hide here for an hour, then they turned down the lights and went to a different part of the museum. Now forty minutes had passed and nothing had happened.

"Seriously, guys," Bess said. "My foot is asleep, and I have to go to the bathroom. I had a whole glass of lemonade and—"

"Shhhhh!" George said again. She covered

Bess's mouth with her hand. Then she pointed to the far end of the hall. The curtain moved. A hand popped through, then two shadowy figures entered the room. One knelt down on the floor.

Nancy ran to the light switch. She turned it on, and the entire room came into view. There, right in the doorway, were two girls in Bensonhurst Academy uniforms. Their maroon cardigans were tied around their waists. One of the girls had both hands on the ground.

"Looking for something?" Nancy asked.

That girl shot straight up, then put her hands behind her back.

"N-no . . . w-we . . . were j-just . . . ," the other girl stuttered.

"Were you looking for this?" George asked. She pulled the coin purse from her pocket and held it in the air.

Nancy recognized the blond-haired girl as Melody Price. She was one of the most popular girls at Bensonhurst Academy. Nancy had seen her during the annual homecoming day parade. Melody was always on the front of the float, waving to all the people crowded on the sidewalk. Now she looked scared, her cheeks a deep pink.

"Um . . . why?" Melody asked.

George walked over to them, holding the purse in her hand. "We were hoping you could help us," she said.

"Can you tell us when you dropped the purse? Did you come in here for a reason?" Nancy asked.

Melody twirled a strand of her hair. "We took a wrong turn, that's all," she said. "We thought our class was in here, but they weren't."

Bess took out her sketch pad and wrote down a few notes. "How could they have possibly taken a wrong turn?" she whispered to George. "There were construction signs everywhere."

The girl with the braid sighed. "Can we have Melody's purse now? We told you everything we know."

As George passed them the purse, Nancy

tried one more question. "Did you see anything strange when you were in here? What time would you say you dropped it?"

Melody looked at her watch. "Maybe about two hours ago. Somewhere around six o'clock. I didn't see anything. Did you, Lena?"

"Nothing," Lena said.

"We ask because this sculpture was broken right around six fifteen," Bess said, looking at her notes. She pointed to the pieces on the ground. "We're trying to figure out who is responsible. So, if you saw anything, it might help us."

"Whoa. . . . I didn't notice that," Lena said. She looked at the cracked head on the floor.

"That's so weird. It was fine when we left," Melody said. "We must've been in the classroom by six fifteen. If you don't believe me, I can show you the ink drawing. My teacher has it somewhere."

Lena kept staring at the broken sculpture. "It definitely didn't look like that when we were here," she said.

Bess looked over her notes. The sculpture was broken somewhere around six fifteen, but both the girls said they'd left the room before that. It must have happened right after they went through. "Was there anyone else around? Maybe in another room or in that hall?" Bess pointed to the side doors.

Melody's eyes went wide. "Now that you mention it . . . there were two men in the room next door. They were painting or hammering or something. I remember we passed them on the way out."

Nancy looked at her friends. "Two more witnesses," she said. "If Melody and Lena didn't see anything, maybe they might have."

Lena looked bored. She kept undoing the end of her braid, then braiding it again. "Can we go now?" she asked.

Melody hooked her arm through Lena's elbow. "Yeah, we were supposed to meet the rest of our class five minutes ago."

"You can go," George said. "But we might

need your help later, and there may be more questions."

Melody rolled her eyes as she walked out of the hall. "Fine, but we told you everything."

Bess looked down at the list of notes she had made, then smiled. Even Melody couldn't shake her good mood. Maybe they didn't have answers, but they had another tip to go on. That was good enough for her.

"Two witnesses down," Bess said. "And two more to go. Come on. Let's see if we can find those workers they mentioned!"

Then she started off into the next hall, waving for George and Nancy to follow her.

Chapter Six

Two ... Suspects?

It took Nancy, Bess, and George a few minutes to find the room Melody and Lena were talking about. They had to make two left turns to get to it, weaving behind the sculpture hall. They pushed past a plastic sheet. Inside, two men were painting the walls a dark blue.

"You girls aren't supposed to be in here," said a round guy with freckles. His nose had a blue smudge on it. "Can't you see this place is under construction? Gallery isn't open for another three weeks."

A thin man with a mask over his face ran a roller up the wall. "Yeah! No one's allowed in here!" he shouted through his mask.

Nancy stepped forward. Bess and George were at her sides. All around them were different sculptures covered in clear plastic sheets. "We have to ask you a few questions," she said.

"Questions about what?" The man pulled his mask off.

"That sculpture that broke down the hall," Bess said. She opened her sketch pad, ready to write down what the men had to say. "Did you hear anything around six fifteen? Any sounds next door?"

The round man scratched his nose, getting even more blue paint on his face. "We were painting, and there was this loud thud. I could hear it on the other side of the wall, but I didn't know what it was."

The man with the mask nodded. "It was strange. We were going to call the guard, but then we saw her run past." He pointed out the arched doorway.

Nancy looked through the clear sheet that covered the entrance. She could see a few shapes beyond it. Rita must have passed them as she went through the sculpture hall—but did the suspect pass them as well? "So, Rita ran that way, toward the sculpture hall. Did you see anyone else run past?"

"No," the man with the mask said. "We were here all day. Don't know much more than that."

Bess scribbled some notes down. "Did you see anything else unusual tonight?"

As the men thought about it, Nancy looked around the room, searching for anything that seemed strange. There were sheets on the floor, some rollers, and paint. If the men were here all day, the suspect probably didn't come through.

The man with the mask started painting again, turning the wall blue. "I don't think so."

"No, there was!" the round man said. "Don't you remember those two girls?"

45

Bess leaned over to Nancy. "Two girls?" she whispered. "Do you think it could be Melody and Lena?"

"What did they look like?" Nancy asked.

The man with the mask pointed to the sculpture hall. "They were wearing matching uniforms. One had a long brown braid. We found them climbing on the scaffolding right by where that sculpture was."

The round man laughed, smacking a blue handprint onto his leg. "That's right. I would bet you a hundred bucks those girls had something to do with it. We went in, and yelled at them. We told them to get down, but they wouldn't listen."

George nudged Nancy in the side. "They said they'd just gone in and out. They said they'd made a wrong turn."

Nancy knew they were onto something. "How long were they there?" she asked the men.

"Fifteen minutes, maybe twenty," the man with the mask said. "They were hiding up there. We came back in here to finish, and then we were going to get the guard to get them down."

"But then we heard that thud," the round man added.

Nancy perked up. "So, you're saying you heard the thud right around the time you saw the girls on the scaffolding?"

"Yup," the man said. Then he picked up a roller and went back to work.

"Do you know what this means?" Bess said. She was nearly shrieking she was so excited. "They lied to us."

"And if they lied to us," George added, "they must have something to hide."

Nancy couldn't help but smile. Normally, she would be upset that someone lied to her, but this was the best news she'd heard all night. Melody and Lena had just gone from witnesses to suspects. Had the Clue Crew solved this case already?

ChaPTER SEVEN

Lights Out

Bess scribbled down everything the two men said. She wrote *SUSPECTS* in capital letters and drew a line underneath. Right below she wrote *Bensonhurst Academy students: Melody and Lena.*

George took one last look around the room. "And you didn't see anyone else in here? No one came through at all today?"

The man with the freckles put his hand on his chin. "No one came through here . . . ," he said. "Oh! That's not right.

Sometime before dinner there was one lady, a woman with black hair."

"That's right," the man with the mask said. "She was looking for someone. But she came through before we saw the girls on the scaffolding."

Bess wrote that down too. "If she came through before you saw the girls, then maybe that was a little before six o'clock?"

The man with the freckles nodded. "That sounds about right."

"What did she look like?" George asked. "Besides the black hair."

The man with freckles pointed through the plastic sheet over the doorway. "It's hard to see much through that, but she did have black hair."

"I think she was wearing red," the other man added. "Something red."

"And that's all you remember?" Nancy asked. Witnesses had a funny way of doing this. They'd sometimes say that they couldn't remember anything else, but there was usually something. It never hurt to ask one last time.

"Oh! The person she was looking for was named Genie."

George smiled at Nancy. "Good detective work," she said. "That could be important."

Bess wrote down all the last details as the girls headed toward the museum restaurant. "We have to find Melody and Lena," Bess said. "They must have something to do with this. They were there at almost the exact same time the sculpture was broken."

Nancy doubled her pace. She could see the entrance to the restaurant up ahead. It was time to question Melody and Lena again, but could the Clue Crew get them to confess?

"You have to let me explain," Melody began. Miss Alcott and Nancy, Bess, and George stood in front of Melody, Lena, and Mr. Porter, Bensonhurst Academy's art teacher. He was a little older than Miss Alcott, with long hair tied back in a ponytail.

The restaurant was nearly empty. The other River Heights kids had gone to the great hall with another chaperone to get ready for the sleepover. The museum flicked the lights several times, telling everyone it was about to close.

Miss Alcott took a deep breath. "Can you tell us why you were in the sculpture hall when it was closed? The workers next door saw you there playing on the scaffolding."

"Is that true?" Mr. Porter asked.

Lena bit her bottom lip. "We were there for a little while. . . ."

"The tour was boring," Melody whined. She looked so different from the girl Nancy and her friends had spoken to a half hour before. Her cheeks were red, and she seemed like she might cry.

"We were just trying to have some fun," Lena added.

Mr. Porter put his hands on his hips. "What happened in there? This is a museum. You can't wander around the halls without a teacher."

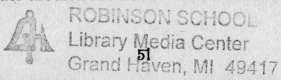

"We snuck away from the tour for a little bit. We were hiding on the scaffolding, playing hangman. Then when we left, I must've dropped my purse. That's all. We didn't do anything to that statue!"

"We didn't even go near it," Lena added. "It was fine. When we left, it wasn't broken. There wasn't anything unusual at all."

A security guard walked up and down the tables, clearing out the restaurant. "Closing time," he said. "If your class is sleeping over, you should report to the medieval armor wing."

"You're admitting to being in the hall at the time the statue was broken," Mr. Porter said. "I have to tell Mr. Whimbley. We can't let the River Heights students pay for this when they weren't even there."

Melody's eyes filled with tears. "We didn't do it though," she said. "Please. I promise. I can prove we're telling the truth."

She pulled a sheet of paper that was folded from her pocket. Across the top was a picture of a hangman and then spaces beneath. The words "SIMON CROSS IS BOOOOORING" were filled in.

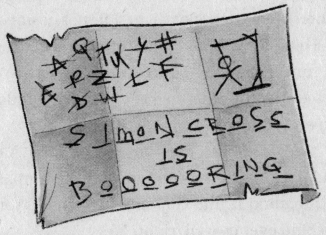

"You were there though, and you lied about it," Miss Alcott said. "Even if you were only playing hangman, how can my students be blamed for this? None of us set foot in that hall. You have to tell Mr. Whimbley."

Lena kept shaking her head. "But, Mr. Porter, we were already in the museum classroom by the time the sculpture broke. We were already working on our ink drawings. You can check the pile—I made one."

"Is that true?" Miss Alcott asked. She looked to Mr. Porter. "Are you certain they were there?"

"The class was so big—" Mr. Porter said. "There were twenty of them. I'm not positive."

The security guard at the other end of the restaurant flicked the lights several times. "We're closed. Head to the medieval wing. We're locking everything up!"

"Let's sort this out tomorrow," Miss Alcott said, looking at the woman with the harp. She was loading it into a giant black case. "You're sleeping over as well, right?"

Mr. Porter nodded. "On the east side of the hall," he said. "Let's talk in the morning." Then he strode ahead of them, Melody and Lena trailing behind. The Clue Crew could still hear Melody and Lena even as they turned the corner.

"I swear we didn't do this, Mr. Porter," she said. "I swear."

Nancy, Bess, and George walked beside Miss Alcott. They'd never seen her so angry before. "I know they broke that statue," she said. "Why else would they lie to you? And now River Heights is getting blamed for it."

They strode into the medieval armor hall. The room was lined with helmets and tin suits. One whole wall was covered in giant silver swords. There, in the center, was a statue of a horse with armor, just like Miss Alcott said.

Most of the class was already lying on the marble floor in their sleeping bags. Some were reading. Others were huddled together talking about the mystery of the broken sculpture.

The other adult on the trip was Beth Derth's mom, though she'd spent most of the time setting up the sleeping area and arranging the dinner at the restaurant. She was passing out extra pillows and blankets to anyone who wanted one. She also passed Nancy, Bess, and George their sleeping bags and backpacks. "Any luck?" she asked, looking from Miss Alcott to them.

"We think we know who did it," Miss Alcott said. "We'll have to talk to Mr. Whimbley tomorrow morning."

Then Miss Alcott and Mrs. Derth walked away, whispering something Nancy couldn't hear. Nancy plopped down on the marble floor. "I don't know," she said, rolling out her sleeping bag. "Something doesn't seem right."

She looked at the other end of the hall. Melody and Lena were crying to some of their friends. One girl rested her hand on Melody's back, trying to make her feel better. "I swear," Melody kept saying. "No one believes us. Just because we were there, it doesn't mean we did anything wrong."

Nancy's couldn't stop watching them. They seemed so sure they hadn't done anything wrong. Was it really all an act?

Bess slipped into her sleeping bag, curling it up around her chin. The lights dimmed in the medieval armor hall. "I know, Nancy," she agreed. "I just can't figure out what doesn't seem right."

"Melody and Lena really seem upset," George added.

Nancy leaned back on her pillow. Her instincts were telling her something was off. As much as Miss Alcott was sure Melody and Lena broke the sculpture, it didn't quite make sense. There had to be something the Clue Crew had missed.

"If they're not lying, then the statue was fine when they left the hall," Nancy whispered. "So it was broken after."

"Which means it couldn't have been the

woman with the black hair who ran through," Bess added. "The men who were painting said she walked past before they discovered Melody and Lena."

"Right," George said. She rubbed her forehead, more frustrated than ever. "But that means if Lena and Melody didn't do it, we don't have a single suspect left. We have to start over from scratch."

Nancy stared up at the domed ceiling. This was one of their trickiest cases yet. She knew Melody and Lena were the closest answer they had, but they couldn't let them get in trouble for something they didn't do. Miss Alcott was convinced, but she hadn't seen all the evidence. Maybe they hadn't seen all the evidence either. Was there something back there in that room?

"Let's sleep on it," Nancy said, turning to her friends. "And tomorrow, before we do anything, we'll go back to the sculpture hall for a second look."

ChaPTER EiGhT

One Last Clue

"I couldn't sleep last night," Nancy said.

"I know," Bess moaned. She rubbed her head. "Robby and Kevin kept making noises and were laughing all night!"

George walked a few steps in front of them, turning left toward the sculpture hall. "Those creepy armor men scared me! They looked like they'd come to life at any moment."

The museum was already full with visitors. A few groups walked around with maps, while another class moved through on a tour. The guide kept waving a red flag in the air, trying to keep everyone together.

"You guys!" a voice called somewhere behind them. "Wait up!"

Melody ran after them. She was holding two papers in her hand. She passed them to Nancy. "We found the ink drawings we did in class last night. See? This should prove that we weren't there when the sculpture broke." She pointed to her name at the bottom of the sheet. Lena's name was written on the other one.

"Thanks for these," Nancy said.

Melody grabbed Nancy's hand. "I'm sorry I lied to you yesterday, but you have to believe us. If I knew anything else, I would've told you, but I don't. I can't explain how the statue broke. I just know we didn't do it."

Nancy felt bad for Melody, but even the ink drawings couldn't prove anything. Melody and Lena could have made them this morning or put their names on them to say they'd been in the classroom at the time that the statue fell. The Clue Crew needed to find more clues . . . more facts. "We're working on it," Nancy said.

"We'll tell you as soon as we have any news."

Then she started back down the hall with Bess and George. When they reached the sculpture hall, everything seemed different. It was funny how returning to a scene could show you new things.

"I knew it," Nancy said. "Look how high this podium is. It's higher than my shoulder."

George circled it. "You're right," she said. "It would be really hard for any of us to knock it over. It doesn't seem like Melody and Lena could."

Bess stuck her head under the giant tarp, and then she disappeared under it for a few minutes. Nancy and George could see her moving beneath it.

"I found something! Another clue!" Bess yelled. She popped out, holding a piece of paper and a pencil.

"Do you think that's what Melody and Lena were writing with?" George asked.

"It at least proves what they were saying.

They were in here, hiding under the tarp. They were playing a game," Bess said.

Nancy looked at where Melody and Lena had been hiding, then back where the sculpture was. "It's too far away for them to have jumped off and knocked it over. They couldn't have climbed down and kicked it. It just doesn't make any sense."

The girls circled the room again. George peered under a few sheets covering some sculptures. Bess looked out the doorway, trying to figure out how the suspect came in. Nancy studied the ceiling for a long time. There was a light right above the broken sculpture, but that was all.

"There has to be something we're missing," George said. She peeked under another sheet.

Nancy took one last walk around the sculpture, and that's when she saw it. Even though most of the red dust had been swept up, there was a little bit still in the corner. "Over here," she said, pointing to the corner. "That's so strange. . . ."

The girls leaned over to see. A patch of the white floor still looked pink. But there, in the center, was a footprint. "What is that?" Bess asked.

George inched closer. It wasn't a boot or a sneaker, not anything the kids or the janitor would wear. It looked like a fancy high heel, like the ones her mom wore to work. "Look at how small it is. That's the front of the shoe and that's the high heel." She pointed to the dot behind it. "But why would someone be walking around here with high heels on? It must've been an adult."

"Definitely," Nancy said. "And she came through after the sculpture broke, because the dust was already here."

Almost as soon as she said it, Bess's eyes opened wide. She inched closer to a podium in the corner, leaning down to look at something. She picked up a tiny red feather, showing Nancy and George. "Look! What do you think this is?"

Nancy shot up straight. "I didn't notice that before. It looks like it's from something . . ."

George pinched it between her fingers. "It's definitely not from an animal," she said. "The color is too weird. It's been dyed."

Nancy cupped her hand over her mouth. "The woman in red. The one with the dark hair who was looking for Genie. Do you think this has to do with her? Maybe this was on something she was wearing?"

"It's hard to say for sure," Bess said. "But it's the only clue we have."

"We have to find her," Nancy said.

"How?" George asked. "She was wearing red yesterday, but she could be wearing anything today. She probably isn't even here. What are the chances she would come to the museum two days in a row?"

Bess let out a sigh. "You're right," she said. "It'll be impossible to find her now."

"If we can't find her, maybe we can figure out who Genie is," Nancy said. "We have to at least try."

Nancy glanced at her watch. They didn't have much time before they had to meet Mr. Whimbley, Miss Alcott, Mr. Porter, Melody, and Lena at the front entrance. "Come on," she said, waving at her friends behind her. "Let's go through the museum one last time. Look out for anything unusual. Anything at all . . ."

CHAPTER NINE

The Great Meela

Nancy and her friends searched the medieval armor room, asking if anyone had met a woman with black hair and a red outfit. They asked every guard if they knew anyone named Genie. They looked through the impressionist wing. They studied every person sitting at the museum restaurant. They'd spent over an hour wandering around, calling out "Genie!" Time was running out.

"It feels hopeless," George said. They walked through the modern art wing one last time, taking in all the strange paintings.

Nancy bit her bottom lip. They always solved the cases they worked on, but this one was tricky.

They had two suspects that they didn't believe did it. Would Melody and Lena get in trouble anyway? What would Mr. Whimbley say when he found out Melody and Lena had been there?

They were nearly at the end of the hallway when Nancy finally saw whom they'd been searching for. "Do you see what I see?" she asked her friends.

George's mouth dropped open. Standing in front of the *Wild* exhibit was a woman in pointy high heels. Over her dress, she wore a red satin cape with feathers around the collar. She had black hair that stuck up in a hundred directions. A tour group crowded around her.

"My name is Meela Deetana, and this is my exhibit *Wild*. It was inspired by nature," she said. "I wanted to show a live animal in a bleak landscape. I wanted to prove how lonely life can be."

Nancy grabbed George's arm. "It's her! That's the woman we've been looking for. She must wear that cape all the time."

The tourists crowded around, some putting their hands against the glass. Inside the room was the ostrich. It ran back and forth in front of the black canvas.

"Look how tall it is," Bess whispered. "It must be seven or eight feet."

Nancy nodded. She knew what Bess was trying to say. Meela was too thin and short to be able to move the sculpture. But the bird was gigantic.

"You're right. That bird is tall enough to knock down a sculpture," Nancy said. "I'm sure of it."

After a few minutes, Meela stepped to the side of the exhibit. A woman with leopard-print pants went up to her, saying how incredible the exhibit was. When she was done, the girls stepped forward.

"Excuse me," Nancy said. "We wanted to ask you a few questions about your exhibit."

"Why of course," Meela said. "What would you like to know?"

Bess flipped through her sketch pad and smiled. She knew exactly what to ask. "What is the ostrich's name?"

Meela laughed. "Are you serious? You want to know the bird's name?"

George knew exactly what Bess was thinking. "Yes! We definitely do."

"That is my Genie," she said, tapping her bright red nails on the glass. "Sweet little Genie."

Nancy started to see how all the clues fit together. The men had seen the woman with black hair run through, looking for someone named Genie. It had happened right around the time the sculpture had been toppled over. The print in the dust seemed to prove it was true. Who else would have been tall enough to knock into the sculpture? How long had the bird been out of its pen?

"We're asking because you were seen looking for Genie around the same time a sculpture was broken," Nancy said. "Do you know anything about that?"

Meela's face went pale. "I don't know what you're talking about. Genie never goes out of the glass cage."

"But where was she when we walked through last night?" Bess asked. "She wasn't in there."

Meela took a deep breath. "I don't know what you're talking about. I had nothing to do with that sculpture. I can't believe you would accuse me!"

Almost as soon as she said it, the crowd behind them gasped. Two boys banged against the glass. "Look! What's that bird doing?" one boy yelled.

Genie had her head down. Her whole body was shaking. "Genie! What's wrong?" Meela cried. She pulled a key chain from her belt, trying to unlock the side door to the exhibit. But before she could even get the key in the lock, the ostrich coughed.

A tiny red thing came out of her mouth. It was covered with spit. "Ewww!" the little boy yelled. "What is that?"

"I think I know what it is," Nancy said, looking through the glass. It was shaped like an ear—a clay ear.

Meela looked embarrassed. "I swear I can explain," she said. She waved the girls into an empty gallery. "Please, come with me. I don't want anyone to hear."

ChaPTER TEN

Genie's Adventure

Meela looked around the gallery, making sure no one was there. After a deep breath, she finally spoke. "I'd come by the exhibit last night to check up on a few last things. And I love seeing my Genie. She always comes right up to the glass when I visit her. That's what she did this time."

"So, she was inside the exhibit when you saw her?" Nancy asked.

Meela bit her lip. "You see that's the problem," she said. "She *was* inside the exhibit. But then I saw that the painting on the wall wasn't hanging right. So I opened the door to go into the room and—*BAM!* Genie ran right out. She's so big that I couldn't stop her. She took off straight down the hall and disappeared into one of the closed-off rooms."

"We knew you were looking for her," Bess said. "One of the men working in the hall heard you calling her name."

"Oh, it was so terrible!" Meela said, nearly crying. "I was afraid she'd get hurt. She was running so fast. Then she slipped on the marble floor and hit the sculpture in the side, knocking it over. I would've done something to fix it, but I had to get her back in the room."

Nancy looked at her friends. It all made sense now. The giant bird was the only thing big enough and tall enough to knock the statue over. Even if three River Heights kids had tried to do it, they couldn't have. Melody and Lena couldn't have done it either. Mr. Whimbley was only looking for someone to blame.

"We have to tell Mr. Whimbley," Bess said. "We have to explain all this to him."

Meela stomped her pointy high heels on the ground. "We can do no such thing!"

George looked confused. "But why?"

Meela leaned down, looking the girls right in the eye. "If Mr. Whimbley finds out Genie got out of her cage, he'll cancel my exhibit. What then? What am I going to do?"

"But right now he thinks our school is responsible for breaking the statue," Nancy explained. "He wants River Heights school district to pay the museum four thousand dollars to repair it."

Meela kept shaking her head. "But my exhibit . . . ," she said. "What am I going to do?"

Nancy looked at her watch again. It was almost ten o'clock. They'd promised to meet Miss Alcott, Mr. Whimbley, Mr. Porter, Melody, and Lena at the museum's great hall in five minutes. "Please," she said. "Will you at least consider it? Our teacher will get in serious trouble with the school."

Meela covered her face with her hands. "I don't know . . . ," she mumbled. "I just don't know."

Nancy felt a lump in her stomach. She'd promised Miss Alcott they'd find out what happened to the sculpture. But now that they had, Meela had asked them not to tell anyone.

Bess grabbed Nancy's arm. "What should we do?" she whispered.

Nancy looked at Meela, who still had her face in her hands. "I don't know," Nancy said. They had solved the case, but what would happen if they told Mr. Whimbley the truth?

Nancy, Bess, and George walked slowly toward the museum's great hall. They could see Miss Alcott, Mr. Porter, and Mr. Whimbley waiting by the main entrance. Melody and Lena sat on a bench, looking even more upset than they had the night before.

"We have to tell them the truth," Nancy said. She glanced behind her. Meela had said she would think about confessing, but it was almost time to leave. They didn't have time to wait for her.

"We'll tell them what we found," Bess said. She pulled out her sketch pad, opening it to the page with all her notes. "The case is closed. River Heights didn't break the sculpture. We shouldn't have to pay for this."

As the girls got closer to the great hall, they felt nervous. "I hate that we're getting someone in trouble," George said. "It feels wrong."

Miss Alcott stood when she saw them. The rest of the class was crowded behind her, a giant pile of sleeping bags and pillows next to them. "Did you find out anything else?" she asked.

"We know Melody and Lena were telling the truth," Nancy said. Mr. Porter looked much happier, but Miss Alcott looked confused. She kept tugging on one of her feather earrings.

"Who did it then?" she asked. "I've talked to all the students this morning, trying to find out more information. It's no use. No one seems to know what happened."

"I know what happened," Mr. Whimbley said. "I gave you until this morning, which was fair. Now River Heights will have to pay for this."

Nancy looked at her friends. She opened her mouth to speak when a voice interrupted her. "Mr. Whimbley!" Meela called from the down the hall. She was running so fast her red cape flew out behind her. "Mr. Whimbley, I have to tell you something. You can't punish these kids for breaking the sculpture."

"Meela, what do you have to do with all this?" Mr. Whimbley asked. He looked over his glasses at the artist.

"I'm going to pay for the sculpture," Meela said. "Because Genie broke it."

Robby called out from the crowd. "Who in the world is Genie?" he asked.

Kevin laughed.

"She's part of my *Wild* exhibit," Meela said.

She looked annoyed. "Genie, the ostrich, got out of her cage last night and darted down the hall. I tried to stop her, but I couldn't."

Meela went on, explaining the full story to Mr. Whimbley. She told him that she was afraid he'd cancel her show if she told the truth. "You need to know that the River Heights kids didn't do this though. I should've told you sooner."

Mr. Whimbley was silent for a moment. He rubbed the bald spot on the back of his head. "I don't know what to say," he mumbled.

Miss Alcott looked happier than she had the entire field trip. "Maybe you could say that you're sorry?" she asked. "This class is one of the best I've had at River Heights Elementary. They're smart, kind, and talented. And they are definitely not liars."

Mr. Whimbley looked around at all the students huddled beside Miss Alcott. His cheeks turned bright red. "Yes," he mumbled. "I suppose I'm sorry."

"Thank you, Mr. Whimbley," Miss Alcott

said. "And we should all thank Nancy, Bess, and George. Without their help we never would've gotten to the bottom of this."

"High five," Kevin yelled. He ran past Nancy, Bess, and George, making them smack his hand.

"All right," Miss Alcott said. "Time to load up the bus. We should get back soon."

Mr. Whimbley pulled Meela aside, talking to her in a volume Nancy couldn't hear. Then he held up his hand. "Wait! Miss Alcott," he called, "I truly am sorry. If you could stay an hour longer, how about I make it up to your class? Would you like to have ice-cream sundaes in the museum garden?"

"And I would love for all of you to meet Genie," Meela said. "She's really quite sweet."

Miss Alcott looked around at her class. "What do you think?" she asked. "It would be a very early dessert."

"Yes! We have to!" Robby yelled.

Everyone else cheered, but no one cheered

louder than Nancy, Bess, and George. Genie was where she belonged. River Heights Elementary was back to being one of the best schools around. And the Clue Crew had solved yet another case.

"Yes," Nancy said. "I think we definitely deserve ice cream." Then she grabbed her friends and headed to the museum gardens.

CRAZY CLAY

Nancy, Bess, and George spent the day looking at paintings and sculptures at the Simon Cross Art Institute. Now you can make your own priceless sculpture, like the ones they found there. Follow the simple instructions below.

You'll need:

- A mixing bowl
- 1 cup flour
- ¼ cup salt

- ¼ cup water
- Food coloring
- Plastic gloves (optional)
- Glitter (optional)

Directions:
- In the mixing bowl, combine the flour and salt. Then add water.
- Knead and squeeze the dough until it feels like clay. If the clay still feels dry, add more water, a few drops at a time.
- When the clay is just right, add two drops of food coloring of any color. Knead and squeeze the dough again, mixing in the color. (You may want to use plastic gloves for this part. It can be messy!)
- For really crazy clay, mix in glitter.
- Now that you have your clay, it's time to make your sculpture. (You may want to work on a piece of cardboard or plate to make it easier to move.) What will you

create? An elephant, a dog, or a person? A cottage or a castle? Will you sculpt a town with roads, cars, and houses?

- When you're finished, give your sculpture two days to dry. Then voilà! You have your own original piece of art.

Nancy Drew and the Clue Crew®

Test your detective skills with more Clue Crew cases!

FROM ALADDIN • PUBLISHED BY SIMON & SCHUSTER

Break out your sleeping bag and best pajamas. . . . You're invited!

Sleepover Squad

❋ Collect them all! ❋

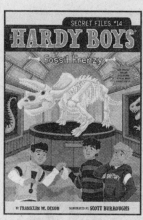

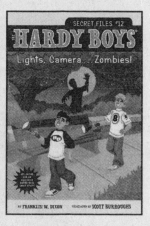
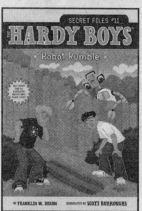
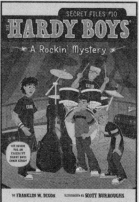

Nancy Drew: Ghost of Thornton Hall

Some Families Keep Deadly Secrets!

Jessalyn Thornton's fateful sleepover at the abandoned Thornton estate was supposed to be a pre-wedding celebration, but the fun ended when she disappeared. While her family searches for clues, others refuse to speak about the estate's dark past. Did something supernatural happen to Jessalyn, or is someone in Thornton Hall holding something besides family secrets?